THIS WALKER BOOK BELONGS TO:

_____

_____

_____

_____

For
Tom Deering
who came with
his bears
M.W.

For Sarah
P.D.

First published 1994 by
Walker Books Ltd, 87 Vauxhall Walk, London SE11 5HJ

This edition published 1996

10 9 8 7 6 5 4 3 2 1

Text © 1994 Martin Waddell Illustrations © 1994 Penny Dale

The right of Martin Waddell to be identified as author of this work has been
asserted by him in accordance with the Copyright, Designs and Patents Act 1988.

This book has been typeset in Stempel Schneidler.

Printed in Hong Kong

British Library Cataloguing in Publication Data
A catalogue record for this book is available
from the British Library.

ISBN 0-7445-4763-6

When the Teddy Bears Came

Martin Waddell ◆ Illustrated by Penny Dale

WALKER BOOKS
AND SUBSIDIARIES
LONDON ◆ BOSTON ◆ SYDNEY

When the new baby came to Tom's house,
the teddy bears started coming.

Alice Bear came in the cot.

Tom kissed Alice Bear and the baby.

Ozzie Bear came with Uncle Jack.

Ozzie Bear had a flag and a hat.

Ozzie Bear sat on a chair,

where he could look after the baby.

Then Miss Wilkins came with Sam Bear
in his sailor suit. Sam Bear sat on the chair
beside Ozzie Bear.

"*I* want to give our baby a bear!" Tom said.
So he gave the new baby his Huggy.
Tom told Mum, "Huggy can look after
our baby now."
Tom put Huggy beside Alice Bear.

Rockwell and Dudley Bear came in a van.

They were squashed a bit.

Tom unsquashed them for the new baby.

Rockwell and Dudley Bear went on the chair

beside Ozzie Bear and Sam Bear.

Gran brought Bodger Bear from her attic.
"That's my Bodger Bear!" Dad said.

Mum said, "Look at
our baby with all
of these bears!"

Tom looked at the bears. Alice Bear, Ozzie Bear, Sam Bear and Huggy, Rockwell and Dudley Bear and Dad's Bodger Bear, all on the couch beside Mum and the baby.

"There's no room for *me*," Tom said to Mum.

Mum smiled and said, "Come here, Tom, and sit on my knee. You and I can look after the bears. It's Dad's turn to look after the baby."

And that's what they did.
When the new baby
came to Tom's house
they all took it in turns
to look after the bears …

and together they all looked after the baby.

MORE WALKER PAPERBACKS
For You to Enjoy

ROSIE'S BABIES
by Martin Waddell/Penny Dale

Winner of the Best Book for Babies Award
and Shortlisted for the Kate Greenaway Medal

"Deals with sibling jealousy in a very convincing way." *Child Education*

0-7445-2335-4   £4.50

ONCE THERE WERE GIANTS
by Martin Waddell/Penny Dale

The story of a girl's development from infancy to motherhood.

"Deeply satisfying to read and reread ... delicately-drawn,
nicely realistic domestic scenes." *The Observer*

0-7445-1791-5   £4.99

OWL BABIES
by Martin Waddell/Patrick Benson

On a tree in the woods, three baby owls, Sarah and Percy and Bill,
wait for their Owl Mother to come home.

"Touchingly beautiful... Drawn with exquisite delicacy...
The perfect picture book." *The Guardian*

0-7445-3167-5   £4.50

Walker Paperbacks are available from most booksellers, or by post from B.B.C.S., P.O. Box 941, Hull, North Humberside HU1 3YQ

24 hour telephone credit card line 01482 224626

To order, send: Title, author, ISBN number and price for each book ordered, your full name and address,
cheque or postal order payable to BBCS for the total amount and allow the following for postage and packing:
UK and BFPO: £1.00 for the first book, and 50p for each additional book to a maximum of £3.50.
Overseas and Eire: £2.00 for the first book, £1.00 for the second and 50p for each additional book.
Prices and availability are subject to change without notice.